Chitraka

(Shuh-TRA-kuh)

A Challenged Cheetah Tale

Africa, land of savannahs and plains,
Big cats still live there, some without manes.

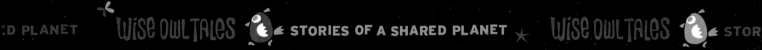

Wise Owl Tales are written in rhyme,
Of animal friends who need our time.

Realistic fiction, stories told,
In nature's settings, tales unfold.

For thoughtful people who understand,
To help the animals, we need a plan.

Books for readers, young to old,
The future of the world we hold.

Our planet Earth is what we share,
Wise Owl Tales, for those who care.

Copyright © 2013 by Wise Owl Tales, LLC
www.wiseowltales.com
Library of Congress Control Number: 2013930647
ISBN 9781939144171
Printed in the U.S.A.

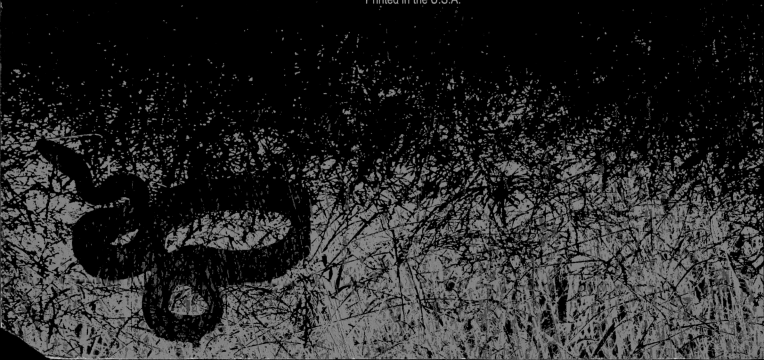

Cheetahs, considered the fastest on land,
Are now in a plight they don't understand.

Chitraka's the name of a young cheetah cat,
She's not a fighter, she avoids combat.

Chitraka is slender, her waist very small,
She's built like a greyhound, long legs and all.

Her short, tan fur is covered in spots,
Round and black, they look like big dots.

Chitraka's eyes are shiny and bright,
Set high on her head, she has excellent sight.

Black tear marks run from her eyes to her mouth,
They protect her from sunlight so strong in the south.

Chitraka's tail is wrapped in dark rings,
A bushy white tuft marks the end as it swings.

Her long tail, like her body, is built for high speeds,
It acts as a rudder, to steer if she needs.

Grasslands, bushlands and wide open spaces,
Are some of Chitraka's favorite places.

But Chitraka has a problem this year,
With three babies to care for, no food is her fear.

She's all on her own as her mate has moved on,
Her young cubs need her from dusk until dawn.

On their necks a mantle of long downy fur,
Camouflages the cubs while they're small and unsure.

Into the morning Chitraka goes out,
She finds a low rock from which she can scout.

Her spots keep her hidden in the high and dry grass,
She's a hunter with skills considered first class.

Chitraka is patient, she stays close to the ground,
She scans the horizon till the right food is found.

Her prey is antelope, gazelle and hare,
But only the sick, weak or old can she snare.

With the sun beating down, she waits by the hour,
Thoughts of her cubs give her strength and willpower.

When the time is just right, she gathers up speed,
Chitraka's so fast, there is no time to heed.

Within a minute it's over, her hunt a success,
The cubs will eat due to her skill and finesse.

Chitraka feels lucky, today there is food,
It's a hard job to find enough for her brood.

Back home with her cubs she gives them their meal,
But she has concerns she doesn't reveal.

She worries that things just don't seem right,
Each year fewer prey she's able to sight.

Chitraka is challenged, her habitat changing,
The future looks bleak, the problems wide-ranging.

There is less and less land for Chitraka to roam,
As humans continue to take over her home.

There are even more troubles Chitraka's been dealt,
She's wanted by poachers because of her pelt.

Some come for adventure to hunt cheetahs down,
These hunters' prize is her fur golden-brown.

What can we do, we must all surely ask?
Saving the cheetahs is a very big task!

It starts with people and education,
Working together for conservation.

When the cheetahs' value we embrace,
The entire world is a better place.

Chitraka still runs on the African plain,
But cheetahs need help if they are to remain.

North America

Equator

South America

Antarctica

Dedicated to the
Chitrakas of the World

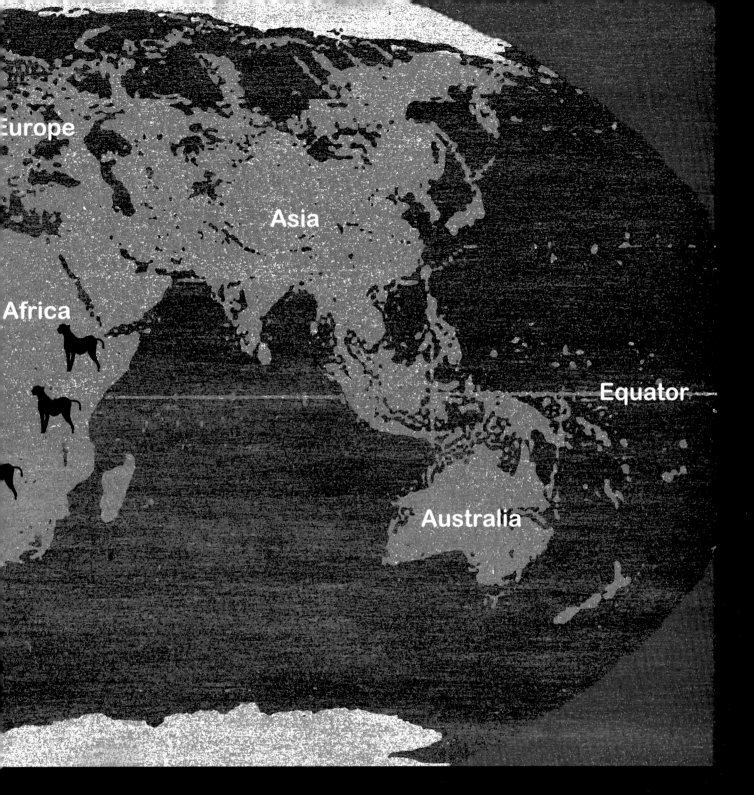

Cheetah Range and Habitat

Cheetahs are found in the southern and eastern parts of Africa. The largest remaining population is in the country of Namibia.

Their range historically included India and Iran, but few remain in those countries.

Cheetah habitat includes semi-desert, grasslands, savannahs and scrubland with thick brush and open flat land.

Glossary
and
Cheetah Facts

Africa - a continent in the Eastern Hemisphere; cheetahs live in the southern and eastern parts of Africa, primarily in the country of Namibia

bleak - dreary, hopeless or gloomy; animals that cheetahs rely on for food are declining in number as their habitat is taken over by man

brood - a group of young from the same family; cheetahs can have up to nine cubs but the average is three to five; cubs live with their mother until they are about 18 months old

cheetah - fastest land mammal, able to accelerate from 0 - 68 mph in 3 seconds, but only for about 1,500 feet; slender with long legs, a deep chest and tan-colored, short spotted fur; considered to be one of the big cats of Africa

Chitraka - a Sanskrit (ancient language of India) word for cheetah; the name also means painted as in painted spots

conservation - to preserve or protect from loss or destruction; organizations in Africa, India and the United States have enacted legislation to try to protect cheetahs

endangered - in danger of extinction; cheetahs are considered endangered

finesse - to do something with grace, mastery or skill; cheetahs are not strong or aggressive and must rely on speed and skill for survival

greyhound - a tall, slender dog with long legs and the ability to run very fast

habitat - the natural home or environment of an animal; one of the biggest problems for cheetahs is declining habitat

heed - to pay attention to something; to use caution

horizon - a point where the earth and sky appear to meet in the distance

mantle - a cloak or cover; baby cheetahs have a mantle of fur which extends from their necks to mid back; the mantle is shed as the cheetah gets older

mate - one of a pair of animals that live together; cheetah males do not stay with the female or help in raising the cubs

pelt - the skin or hide of an animal with fur; a cheetah's fur is valued by poachers

plain - a large, flat area of land with few trees; cheetah habitat includes plains and savannahs

plight - an unhappy situation or predicament; some scientists believe cheetahs may not survive as a species

poacher - someone who hunts animals illegally; killing cheetahs is against the law in many countries, but poachers kill for trophies or for money on the black market

prey - an animal that is caught and eaten by another; a cheetah's prey includes ground birds, antelope, gazelle, hare, wildebeest and zebra; they watch for animals that are slower due to age or injury

reveal - to declare or make known

rudder - something that controls direction; at 2.5 feet in length, a cheetah's long, flexible tail is almost half as long as its body and is used to change direction in midair when chasing prey

savannah - a grassy area of land found in subtropical regions

scout - to investigate or observe in order to get information; cheetahs have very good eyesight to scan the horizon for prey; cheetahs hunt in the morning or evening when there is enough light to see but is cooler than midday

snare - to capture or trap; cheetahs chase and knock their prey down, then quickly kill it with a suffocating bite to the under side of the throat; cheetahs must eat immediately after a kill before larger predators take it from them

swell - to increase in number or size; as the population of countries in Africa increases, the need for farmland increases as well

tuft - a bunch or cluster of strands of fur that are attached at one end; the tail of a cheetah is covered in spots forming six to eight rings and ending in a white tuft of fur

willpower - determination, self-control or strength of mind; cheetahs are patient and will wait until their prey is within 50 feet before attacking in order to save their energy

STORIES OF A SHARED PLANET

WISE OWL TALES

What is unique or special about Chitraka's habitat?

Could cheetahs survive in any other habitat? Why or why not?

Does Chitraka's character remind you of anyone you know?

Chitraka is a hunter but not a fighter. How are these characteristics different?

Which verse in the story is most meaningful to you and why?

Can you relate, or make a connection with any situation in the story?

What is the main idea of Chitraka's story?

What aspect of the cheetahs' plight were you not aware of before?

In the story Chitraka has worries and concerns; do you think animals can have these feelings?

What lesson(s) can be learned from Chitraka's story?

What is your opinion about the problems cheetahs face?

The cheetahs' prey are declining; are other animals in Africa facing similar problems?

How can people and cheetahs share the same land?

What are the long-term consequences of a declining habitat for cheetahs?

Do you believe it is important to save cheetahs from extinction? Why or why not?

What solutions do you think will help cheetahs the most?

How does Chitraka's story make you feel?

Do you think cheetahs will continue to survive?

What does the difference between the first and last verse of the story mean to you?

What do you think? Share your answers at www.wiseowltales.com

Wise Owl Tales

 **STORIES OF A SHARED PLANET**

Add to your Wise Owl Tale collection, here are more for your selection.
Visit us at www.wiseowltales.com for books and activities

A story of travel from here to there,
A young armadillo who goes everywhere.
Armando - an Adventurous Nine-Banded Armadillo Tale

A story of hunger and lost habitat,
A mother who hunts but avoids combat.
Chitraka - a Challenged Cheetah Tale

A story of rescue, where kids save the day,
Working together, they don't back away.
Daphina - a Freed Bottlenose Dolphin Tale

A story of creatures walking the shore,
Of tracks left behind, so fun to explore!
Footprints - a Beach Tale

A story of love and gratitude,
An adopted mutt with attitude!
Frank the Tank - an Adopted Dog Tale

A story of hope after despair,
An orphaned gorilla receives loving care.
Gamba - an Optimistic Mountain Gorilla Tale

A story of capture and desolation,
Of rescue, shelter and preservation.
Mali - a Rescued Asian Elephant Tale

A story of change and loss of home,
A hungry family on the roam.
Nanuk - a Hopeful Polar Bear Tale

Pictures and words by Lopez and Burk,
Inspired by nature, love their work.
Learners, teachers and travelers, who
Look at life from the animals' view.